Explore!
EARLY
Islamic
CIVILISATION

Izzi Howell

WAYLAND
www.waylandbooks.co.uk

First published in Great Britain in 2017 by Wayland

Copyright © Hodder and Stoughton Limited, 2017

All rights reserved.

ISBN 978 1 5263 0082 9
10 9 8 7 6 5 4 3 2 1

MIX
Paper from responsible sources
FSC® C104740

Wayland
An imprint of Hachette Children's Group
Part of Hodder & Stoughton
Carmelite House
50 Victoria Embankment
London EC4Y 0DZ

An Hachette UK Company
www.hachette.co.uk
www.hachettechildrens.co.uk

A catalogue record for this title is available from the
British Library

Printed and bound in China

Produced for Wayland by
White-Thomson Publishing Ltd
www.wtpub.co.uk

Editor: Izzi Howell
Designer: Clare Nicholas
Illustrations: Julian Baker
Wayland editor: Hayley Shortt
Consultant: Philip Parker

Picture acknowledgements:
The author and publisher would like to thank the
following agencies and people for allowing these
pictures to be reproduced:

Alamy: FineArt 23b; Bridgeman: Ms Ar 5847 fol.5,
Abu Zayd in the library at Basra, from 'The Maqamat'
(The Meetings) by Al-Hariri, c.1240 (gouache on
paper), Al-Wasiti, Yahya ibn Mahmud (13th Century)/
Bibliotheque Nationale, Paris, France/Archives Charmet/
Bridgeman Images 15t; Dreamstime: Brizardh 7t;
iStock: bluejayphoto 10-11b, ZU_09 13b, numbeos 23t,
powerofforever 27tl; LACMA: The Madina Collection of
Islamic Art, gift of Camilla Chandler Frost (M.2002.1.14)
title page r and 15br, Gift of Nasli M. Heeramaneck
(M.76.174.273) 9b, © Museum Associates The Nasli M.
Heeramaneck Collection, gift of Joan Palevsky (M.86.196)
17, Mr. and Mrs. Allan C. Balch Collection (M.45.3.90)
22; Mary Evans Picture Library: Iberfoto 12, INTERFOTO
/ Bildarchiv Hansmann 13t, Photo Researchers 18 and
19b; Shutterstock: VanderWolf Images cover b, Everett
- Art title page l and 28, BEGY Production 4, Faris.B 5b
and 31, artpixelgraphy Studio 6, Rawpixel.com 8 and 29b,
Jose Ignacio Soto 10t and 32, Martchan 11t, saiko3p 14,
David Herraez Calzada 20, Pikoso.kz 21t, Maatman 21b,
Lilyana Vynogradova 24t, JStone 27tr, JStone 27b, Link
Art 28, Juan Aunion 29t; Stefan Chabluk: 7b and 11b;
TopFoto/The Granger Collection 9t, Wellcome Images:
mpl 5, Wellcome Library, London 15bl; Werner Forman
Archive: Spink and Son Ltd cover tl, Mrs Bashir Mohamed
Collection,London cover tr, British Museum, London
cover cr; Wikimedia: Daderot, Sackler Museum, Harvard
University, Cambridge, Massachusetts, USA 3 and 16,
Walters Art Museum, Acquired by Henry Walters 19.

All design elements from Shutterstock.

Please note:
The website addresses (URLs) included in this book were
valid at the time of going to press. However, because
of the nature of the Internet, it is possible that some
addresses may have changed, or sites may have changed
or closed down since publication. While the author and
publishers regret any inconvenience this may cause to the
readers, no responsibility for any such changes can be
accepted by either the author or the publishers.

Contents

Early Islamic civilisation

Islamic civilisation started in Arabia in the 7th century CE, after the beginning of the religion of Islam (see p6). It later spread across the Middle East, Asia, Africa and Europe, forming a massive empire.

The laws and customs of the early Islamic civilisation were based on the Quran, the holy book of Islam. Muslims believe that the Quran contains the word of God, as revealed to Muhammad ﷺ.

Islamic rulers

The first leader of the Islamic civilisation was the prophet Muhammad ﷺ, who also founded Islam. Later, it was ruled by leaders known as caliphs. The area controlled by a caliph was called a caliphate. The caliph collected taxes from everyone across the empire to pay for new buildings and libraries and to help the sick and the poor.

Education and science

The early Islamic civilisation was very advanced for its time. Most children in the Islamic Empire went to school and many people could read, in contrast with Europe at that time, where many more people were illiterate. During the golden age of Islamic civilisation (750–1258), the caliphs gave huge amounts of money to scholars so that they could write books and study science.

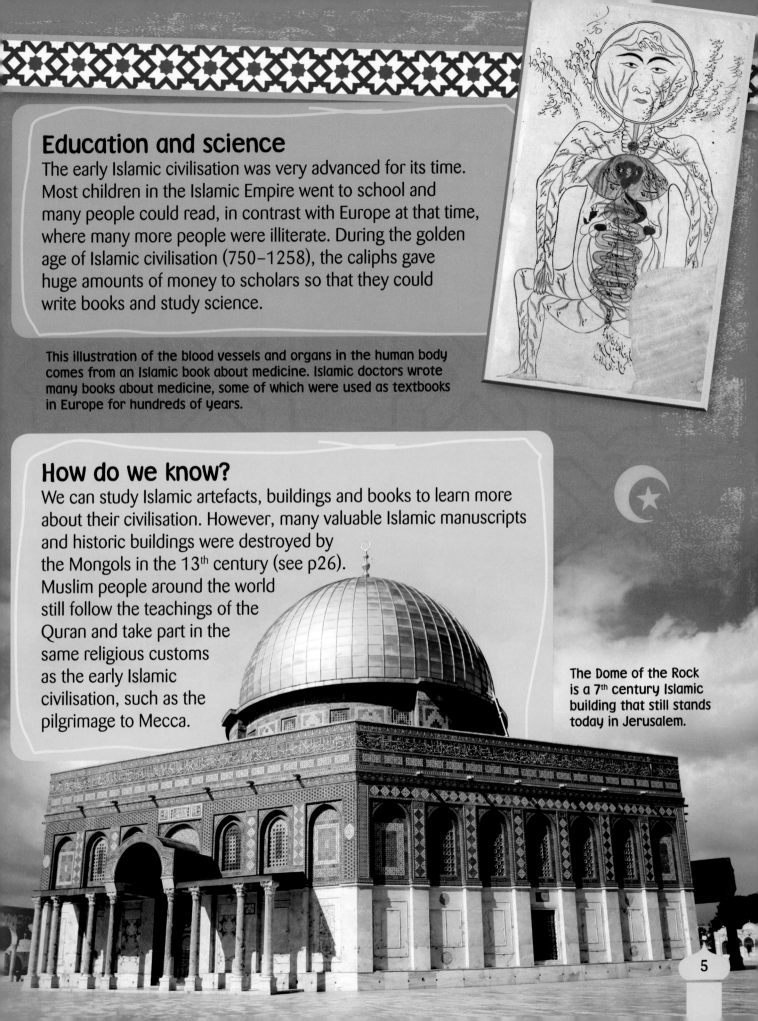

This illustration of the blood vessels and organs in the human body comes from an Islamic book about medicine. Islamic doctors wrote many books about medicine, some of which were used as textbooks in Europe for hundreds of years.

How do we know?

We can study Islamic artefacts, buildings and books to learn more about their civilisation. However, many valuable Islamic manuscripts and historic buildings were destroyed by the Mongols in the 13th century (see p26). Muslim people around the world still follow the teachings of the Quran and take part in the same religious customs as the early Islamic civilisation, such as the pilgrimage to Mecca.

The Dome of the Rock is a 7th century Islamic building that still stands today in Jerusalem.

The beginning of Islam

The first step towards an Islamic civilisation was the founding of the Islamic religion in the 7th century CE. It was started by the prophet Muhammad ﷺ and quickly spread across the Middle East, before expanding across several continents.

The birth of a religion

Muhammad ﷺ was born in the city of Mecca, Arabia, in 570 CE. The people in Arabia at that time lived in separate tribes and followed different religions, such as paganism, Christianity and Judaism. In around 610 CE, Muhammad ﷺ announced that he had received revelations from God. He began to tell others about the word of God, as revealed to him, and people started to follow his religion. His followers were called Muslims.

Today, you can visit the Cave of Hira, the place where it is said that Muhammad ﷺ received his first revelation while praying.

Spreading out

In 622 CE, angry tribes forced Muhammad ﷺ and his followers to leave Mecca. They moved 340 km away to the city of Medina and started a Muslim community there. Eventually, Muhammad's ﷺ followers defeated many local tribes and united them together. Many Arabs changed their religion to Islam.

According to legend, Muhammad ﷺ started construction of the Quba Mosque in Medina as soon as he arrived in the city, making it one of the oldest mosques in the world.

The rise of an empire

When Muhammad ﷺ died in 632 CE, his followers chose a new leader, or 'caliph', meaning 'someone who comes after' in Arabic. The first caliph, Abu Bakr, gathered a large army and began to conquer land outside Arabia. Over the next 100 years, Muslim armies took control of 15 million square km of land across Europe, North Africa, and Asia, creating a massive empire.

This map shows how the Islamic Empire grew from 632 CE to its largest size in 750 CE. After the Rashidun caliphs (632-661), who ruled after Muhammad ﷺ, the empire was ruled by the Umayyad dynasty (661-750) and the Abbasid dynasty (750-1258).

RUSSIA

FRANCE EUROPE

SPAIN
CORDOBA○○GRANADA
MOROCCO

TURKEY

SYRIA IRAQ IRAN
○DAMASCUS ○BAGHDAD

○SAMARKAND
ASIA

CHINA

CAIRO○

EGYPT

MEDINA○

MECCA○ SAUDI
ARABIA

○DELHI

INDIA

AFRICA

INDIAN OCEAN

1000 KM
1000 MILES

■ ISLAMIC CALIPHATE BY 632
■ ISLAMIC CALIPHATE BY 661
□ ISLAMIC CALIPHATE BY 750

ATLANTIC OCEAN

COUNTRIES ARE LABELLED WITH THEIR MODERN NAMES

7

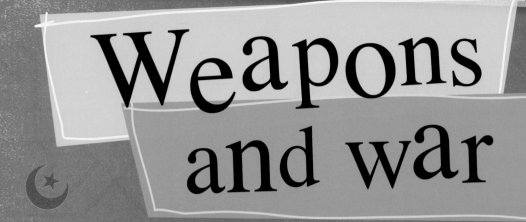

Weapons and war

The Islamic Empire was able to conquer land quickly thanks to its large, well-organised army.

The Islamic army travelled to battle on camels or horses. However, only a small group of soldiers rode during battle.

In control

As the Islamic Empire expanded, their army grew bigger and more powerful. The Islamic army was controlled by generals, who were chosen by the caliph. Many of the men were experienced warriors who fought in many wars and were paid by the state to fight. The caliph used tax money to pay their wages.

On foot

At first, most soldiers in the Islamic army fought on foot with swords, spears and bows. They used their bows at the beginning of battle, firing at their enemy from up to 150 m away. Their long spears and swords were used for hand to hand combat.

Umayyad soldiers wore metal helmets, made from bronze or iron. This statue of a soldier (shown here reflected in a mirror) was made in around 700 CE.

Fighting and riding

Cavalry soldiers that rode horses or camels in battle fought with lances and swords. They did not use bows, as they did not know how to fire a bow while moving. Stopping to use a bow made them vulnerable. At the beginning of the 9th century, Turkish soldiers joined the Islamic army and taught the cavalry how to ride and use bows at the same time.

This plate from the 8th century shows a soldier fighting with a sword on horseback. The first Islamic soldiers used straight swords but over time, they changed to curved swords.

Cities and buildings

There were many large cities across the Islamic Empire. When a new dynasty of caliphs came into power, they usually built a new capital city filled with grand palaces, mosques and gardens.

Across the empire

One of the largest cities of the Islamic civilisation was Córdoba, in southern Spain. In 711, the Umayyad caliphate invaded most of Spain and Portugal. This land was called Al-Andalus. In 756, Al-Andalus split from the rest of the Islamic Empire and made Córdoba its capital city. Mosques, libraries and palaces were built in Córdoba and people came from across the empire to live, study and work.

The Great Mosque of Córdoba was built on the site of a Christian church. When Córdoba was taken over by Christians in 1236, the mosque was turned back into a church but the structure of the mosque can still be seen inside.

The Alhambra palace was built in the Spanish city of Granada by its Muslim rulers. Granada was the last Muslim city in Spain until it was taken by the Christians in 1492.

In the city

Most major cities across the Islamic civilisation were filled with mosques, libraries, schools, bathhouses, theatres, gardens, hospitals, markets and racecourses. Most buildings were made from brick and marble. The caliph and members of his court lived in grand houses with large enclosed courtyards. Poor people lived in simple houses made from mud.

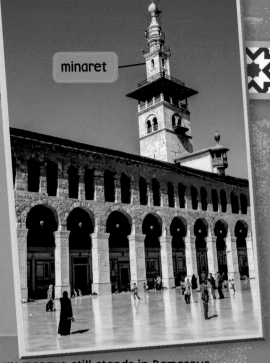

minaret

This 8th century mosque still stands in Damascus, Syria, which was the capital of the Umayyad caliphate. It has many features that are typical of Islamic architecture, such as arches and minarets.

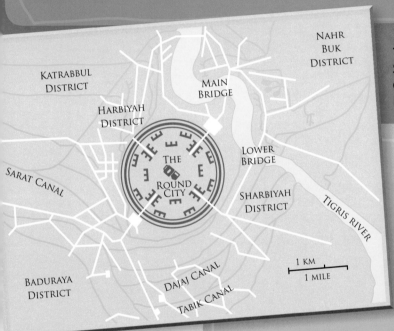

KATRABBUL DISTRICT

HARBIYAH DISTRICT

NAHR BUK DISTRICT

MAIN BRIDGE

SARAT CANAL

THE ROUND CITY

LOWER BRIDGE

SHARBIYAH DISTRICT

TIGRIS RIVER

BADURAYA DISTRICT

DAJAJ CANAL

TABIK CANAL

1 KM
1 MILE

This map shows the layout of Baghdad in the 9th century.

Baghdad

Baghdad was the capital city and cultural centre of the golden age of the Islamic civilisation. Work began on the city in 762 CE on the orders of the Abbasid caliph al-Mansur. It took 100,000 workers four years to complete the city, which became known as the 'round city' because of its circular shape. Baghdad quickly expanded beyond the walls of the round city and by the 10th century, it was the largest city in the world at that time, with over 500,000 inhabitants.

Society

The caliph was the ruler of the Islamic civilisation, but all laws were based on the teachings of Islam. However, people of other religions were welcome to live and work in the Islamic empire.

Different religions

The Islamic civilisation expanded very quickly but it took a while for the religion to spread across the empire. In 750 CE, only 8 of every 100 people in the empire were Muslims. The rest were Christians, Jews or pagans. Eventually, many people chose to become Muslims, but no one was forced to convert. However, people of other religions had to pay a special tax and had fewer rights than Muslims.

Muslims (left), Christians (centre) and Jews (right) usually wore slightly different clothes. Wealthy Muslim women often wore veils, but poor women left their heads uncovered as veils made it hard for them to do physical work.

Laws and customs

Everyone in the Islamic Empire followed Muslim law based on the Quran, also known as shari'a. These laws covered personal and professional aspects of everyday life, from marriages, giving to charity and prayer, to businesses and taxes. As Muslims have to regularly attend mosques to pray, mosques became important meeting points where public announcements were made. Most people celebrated religious events such as Ramadan.

This illustration shows pilgrims taking part in the Hajj (a pilgrimage to Mecca). Islamic law states that all Muslims must make a pilgrimage to Mecca once in their lives, if they are physically able to.

Rich and poor

The wealthiest people in the Islamic civilisation were the caliph and the people at his court who helped him to rule. When they weren't holding meetings, they enjoyed lavish feasts and entertainment provided by musicians and storytellers. Most rich women did not work, but in some parts of the empire, such as Spain, women were educated and could have a wide range of jobs, from tax collector to scholar. Poor people worked as farmers or labourers.

Some of the most famous stories from the time of the Islamic civilisation are from a story collection called *One Thousand and One Nights*. This drawing shows Scheherazade, the narrator of the stories.

Education and books

The University of Al Quaraouiyine in Fes, Morocco, is the oldest madrasa (Islamic school) still in use today. It was opened in 859 by a woman called Fatima al-Fihri.

Education and literacy were very important in the early Islamic civilisation, as it was believed that all Muslims needed to read the Quran. Scholars translated old texts and wrote new books, which were stored in huge libraries.

Starting school

During the golden age of Islamic civilisation, there were primary schools in most towns. From the age of six, children studied the Quran and learned how to read and write. However, many poor children could not go to school as they had to work with their parents. Girls usually left school at the age of twelve, but occasionally, girls were allowed to continue with their education alongside the boys at a madrasa. Here, they could study subjects such as medicine, law, history and maths.

This 12th century illustration shows scholars studying and debating in a library.

Books and libraries

Arabic traders learned the secret of papermaking in China and brought it back to the Islamic Empire. Before paper, scholars wrote on expensive, fragile papyrus or animal skin. The arrival of paper meant that books could be made cheaply and quickly. These books were stored in public libraries, the biggest of which was the House of Wisdom in Baghdad. Scholars were paid to translate ancient texts into Arabic and produce their own books for the libraries.

Writing

The main language of the early Islamic civilisation was Arabic, which came from Arabia. Before Islam, there were several slightly different ways to write the Arabic language. When people started writing down the Quran, they began to use the same alphabet so that copies of the book could be read across the empire. As it is forbidden to decorate religious items or places with images of humans or animals, scribes decorated copies of the Quran with beautiful calligraphy and geometric patterns.

This is a page from a copy of the Quran that was made in the 9th century. Unlike our alphabet, Arabic is written from right to left across the page.

Pottery and tiles were also decorated with calligraphy. This jug was made in Iran in the 10th century.

A day in the life

Scribes had an important role in early Islamic society, as there was a high demand for copies of the Quran and other important texts. This fictional diary entry describes what it might have been like to work as a scribe.

Scribes kept their pens in elaborately decorated pen cases. They could afford luxury items as they earned a good salary.

I wake up early, thinking about today's work. The local mosque has just ordered a new copy of the Quran and I am keen to get started. I wash, get dressed and have a quick breakfast of figs and almonds to prepare me for a morning of hard work.

My first job is to make a new pen with a thin nib so that I can decorate the pages with delicate lines and patterns. I take a dried reed and cut across it at an angle. Then I cut a slit across the pointed tip. I take my other pens out of my pen box to check that I have enough for this project.

Scribes sometimes used coloured or perfumed inks. This 10th century manuscript has been written on paper that has been dyed blue.

The ink that I was using yesterday has dried up, so I mix more from soot, hardened tree sap, honey and water. I test out my new pen and it works perfectly! It's time to start working on my new project.

I get out my Quran and start copying the text. I want to honour the scribe that made my Quran so I copy his style of writing as closely as possible. I pour a small amount of powder onto the page when I am done to dry the ink quickly. The mosque would not be happy if I smudged any of the pages of their Quran. When the writing is done, I add some gold details and patterns to the page. The Quran is a holy book so I add these beautiful details to show our respect for it.

The diary entry on these pages has been written for this book. Can you create your own diary entry for another person who lived in an early Islamic city? It could be a caliph or a scientist. Use the facts in this book and in other sources to help you write about a day in their life.

Science and medicine

After studying and translating ancient scientific texts, Islamic scientists went on to make their own discoveries. Caliphs paid for scientists to research many areas of science, including maths, astronomy and medicine.

Seeing the stars

Astronomers studied the sky from observatories, using instruments that they developed themselves. They made maps of the location of the stars and the movements of the Sun, Moon and planets. A good knowledge of mathematics was important, as they had to calculate distances and curves. Islamic astronomers were able to make accurate calculations of the circumference of the Earth and the time it takes for the Earth to move around the Sun.

This illustration shows Islamic astronomers in an observatory, using different astronomical instruments.

This manuscript shows two Islamic doctors preparing medicine from plants.

Health and medicine

Taxes collected across the Islamic Empire paid for hospitals in all major cities. Doctors were well trained and needed to attend medical school before they could start work. By law, nobody could be turned away from a hospital, even if they couldn't pay for treatment. People could also go to pharmacies for medicines made from plants, such as poppies, cinnamon or sandalwood tree bark.

Inventions

As well as astronomical instruments, Islamic scientists developed many new inventions. Some were practical, such as water pumps for farming, while others were just for fun, such as fountains and simple robots. One of the most famous Islamic inventors was al-Jazari. His book, the *Book of Knowledge of Ingenious Mechanical Devices*, contains instructions for over 50 inventions, many of which have been successfully built and tested by modern engineers.

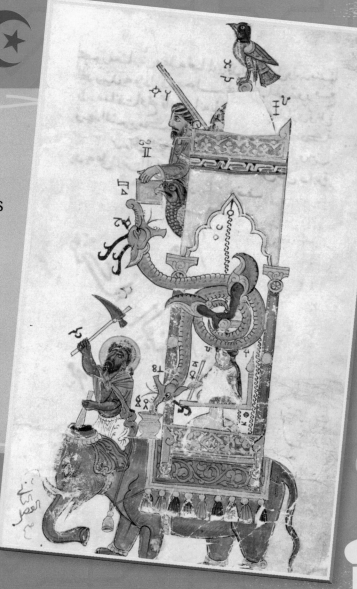

In Al-Jazari's elephant clock, the elephant rider bangs his drum every half-hour to announce the time. It is powered by water and a system of strings.

Farming and food

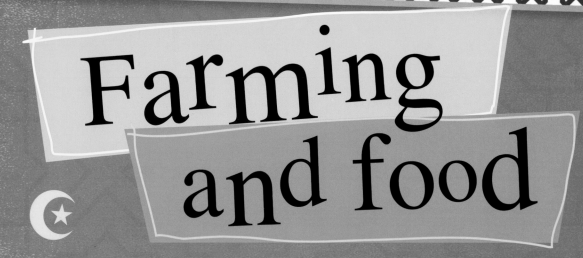

People in the Islamic Empire ate a wide range of foods. Farmers in the empire grew grains, fruits and vegetables, while traders brought exotic ingredients from other countries.

Farming

The people in the Islamic Empire had to farm large areas of land in order to grow enough food to support their population. As the climate in most of their territory was hot and dry, engineers developed clever ways to irrigate the soil so that crops could grow well. Waterwheels and pumps drew water from rivers. The water was carried to the fields by aqueducts and canals.

This Islamic waterwheel known as the Albolafia Mill still stands on the Guadalquivir River in southern Spain. To the left of the wheel is an aqueduct to carry water to the fields.

Crops and orchards

In the fields, farmers grew crops such as wheat, rice and cotton. Fruits, such as figs, pomegranates and oranges, and nuts grew on trees in orchards. Date palm trees were planted in dry areas, as they didn't need much water to grow. In big cities, food markets sold cheeses, sweet pastries, olives and herbs.

Spices from India such as cinnamon and cardamom were popular ingredients. They were expensive, as they had to be imported by traders.

Meat

Muslims across the Islamic Empire followed strict rules about their diet. Pork and alcohol were forbidden. Other types of meat had to be slaughtered in the right way, so that they were halal (allowed to be eaten by Muslims). The most commonly eaten meats were sheep and goat.

Sheep and goats were popular livestock animals as they can live on rocky hillsides – a common type of land across the Islamic Empire.

Trade and travel

During the Islamic civilisation, traders and explorers crossed the Islamic Empire and beyond. Some explorers brought back valuable goods and made maps of distant lands.

Trade

As there was usually peace across the Islamic Empire, merchants could easily transport valuable goods without the risk of attack from enemies. However, for extra protection, they travelled together in groups, known as caravans. Much of the territory of the Islamic Empire is desert, so merchants rode camels, as they can survive for long periods without water. Regions within the empire had their own specialities, such as leather from Spain. Traders also imported pottery and silk from China and gold from Africa.

Syria was well-known for its beautiful glassware, such as this patterned bottle.

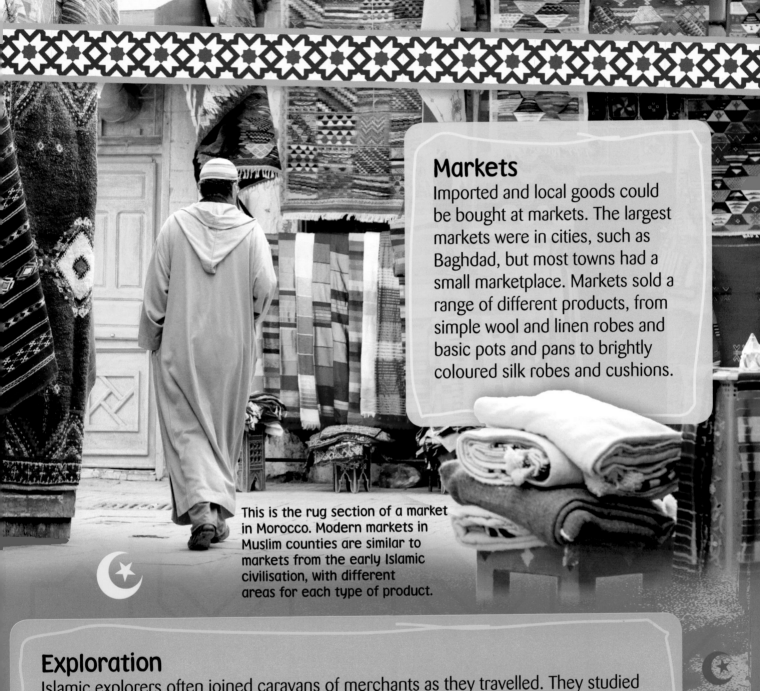

Markets

Imported and local goods could be bought at markets. The largest markets were in cities, such as Baghdad, but most towns had a small marketplace. Markets sold a range of different products, from simple wool and linen robes and basic pots and pans to brightly coloured silk robes and cushions.

This is the rug section of a market in Morocco. Modern markets in Muslim counties are similar to markets from the early Islamic civilisation, with different areas for each type of product.

Exploration

Islamic explorers often joined caravans of merchants as they travelled. They studied the geography of the Islamic territory and the lands beyond it and wrote about the new cultures that they experienced. Some sailed on trade ships, known as dhows, using an instrument called an astrolabe for navigation. One of the best-travelled Muslim explorers was al-Mas'udi (896–956), who visited East Africa and India.

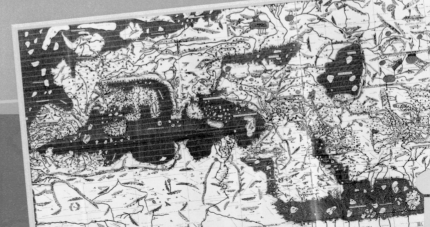

This map is a combination of several maps created by the Islamic map-maker al-Idrisi (1100-1166). At that time, they were the most accurate world maps ever drawn.

Make an Islamic tile design

Islam does not allow figurative art (images of people or animals) on religious objects or places, as they believe that it encourages people to worship things other than God. Instead, they decorate their religious buildings with intricate geometric patterns made out of coloured tiles. You can make your own geometric tile pattern using coloured paper.

A tile wall with a geometric pattern from the Alhambra palace in Granada, Spain.

You will need:

2 pieces of A4 orange paper

2 pieces of A4 purple paper

2 pieces of A4 white paper

scissors

1 A3 piece of coloured card

pencil

ruler

glue stick

triangle template

1 Cut out around 30 triangles from the orange paper, around 20 triangles from the purple paper and around 25 squares from the white paper. The squares should measure 5 cm by 5 cm and each triangle side should measure 5 cm. You can trace this triangle shape and use it as a guide if necessary.

2 Use your pencil and your ruler to mark the centre of the A3 sheet of card. Glue six of the orange triangles around the centre point to form a hexagon shape.

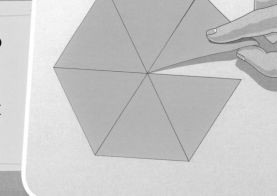

3 Glue one square on each side of the hexagon. Glue purple triangles into the spaces between the squares.

4 Make your tile pattern bigger by adding extra triangles and squares in the pattern shown below.

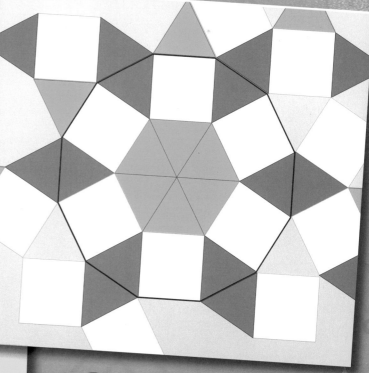

Handy hint
Try using different shapes and colours to make new tile designs.

The end of the empire

The Islamic Empire started to split apart towards the end of the 10th century. However, the Islamic religion and Arabic language lived on and are still practised and spoken today.

Falling apart

One of the first areas to break away from the Islamic Empire was Al-Andalus, which became independently ruled in 756. Over time, more and more regions broke away and by 945, the Abbasids had lost control of most of the empire. At the beginning of the 13th century, a group called the Mongols started to take control of China, central Asia and the Middle East. They reached Baghdad in 1258 and destroyed the city before killing the caliph.

First, the Mongols besieged the city of Baghdad. After its inhabitants surrendered, the Mongols tore down many buildings and libraries, including the House of Wisdom.

The Taj Mahal was built in the 17th century by the leader of the Mughal Empire (a Muslim empire that ruled over India and Afghanistan).

The Taj Mahal has many Islamic architectural features, such as minarets and carved calligraphy and geometric patterns.

Other empires

Many historians think that the destruction of Baghdad was the end of the golden age of early Islamic civilisation. The early Islamic civilisation was followed by several other Muslim empires that rose up across Turkey, Africa and India. The Ottoman Empire, who ruled from Turkey, expanded over southeast Europe, the Middle East and North Africa and lasted from the end of the 13th century to the beginning of the 20th century.

Modern Islam

Today, there are 1.6 billion Muslims living around the world. It is the second largest world religion after Christianity. Some countries, such as Saudi Arabia, have Islam as their official religion and follow shari'a law. However, there are large Muslim communities on every continent, particularly in Africa and Asia. Muslims around the world continue to make valuable contributions to modern science and society, just as in the golden age of Islamic civilisation.

Malala Yousafzai is a famous Pakistani activist for female education and a practising Muslim.

Facts and figures

According to ancient texts, there were 400,000 books in the House of Wisdom in Baghdad. However, it is also reported that one library in Córdoba contained 600,000 books!

At its largest, the Islamic Empire controlled around 10 per cent of the land on Earth.

When Muhammad died in 632 CE, the Islamic army only had 13,000 men. Within 30 years, the caliphate had grown so large that the army was made up of 100,000 men.

The numerals that we use today (1, 2, 3, 4) were introduced to Europe by Islamic mathematicians. Before this, people in Europe used Roman numerals (I, II, III, IV). Islamic mathematicians also introduced the idea of using a circular numeral, 0, to represent zero.

Hygiene was very important in the early Islamic civilisation. Muslims washed themselves before each of their daily prayers and it is believed that people used deodorant and toothpaste. Europeans that lived at the same time only washed a few times every year.

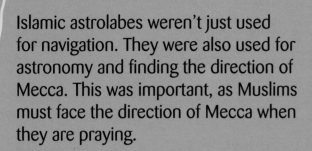

Islamic astrolabes weren't just used for navigation. They were also used for astronomy and finding the direction of Mecca. This was important, as Muslims must face the direction of Mecca when they are praying.

Timeline

570 CE	Muhammad ﷺ is born in Mecca, Arabia.
c. 610	Muhammad ﷺ receives his first revelation from God.
632	Muhammad ﷺ dies and the first caliph, Abu Bakr, takes control.
750	The Islamic Empire is at its height.
756	Al-Andalus splits from the rest of the Islamic Empire.
1258	The city of Baghdad is destroyed by the Mongols.

Glossary

aqueduct A bridge that carries water

artefact An object from the past that reveals information about the people who made it

besiege To surround a place with an army in order to attack it

caliphate The area ruled by a caliph

caliph A Muslim religious and political leader from the past

calligraphy The art of handwriting

CE The letters 'CE' stand for 'common era'. They refer to dates after CE 1.

circumference The distance around something

civilisation A well-organised society

climate The weather conditions in an area

dynasty A series of rulers from the same family

empire A group of countries under the rule of one leader

fictional Made-up or invented

figurative art Art that shows people or objects from real life

geometric With regular repeating shapes and lines

illiterate Describes someone who cannot read or write

irrigate To bring water to fields of crops

manuscript A book or document that has been written by hand

merchant A person who travels around buying and selling goods

minaret A tall, thin tower in a mosque from which Muslims are called to prayer

Mongols A group of people from Central Asia that controlled a giant empire in the 13th and 14th centuries

mosque A Muslim place of worship

nib The pointed end of a pen

paganism A religion in which people worship many gods

pilgrimage A journey made for religious reasons

prophet A person who is believed to have a special power that allows them to say what a god wishes to tell people

revelation A communication from God

scholar A person who studies a subject in great detail

scribe Someone who writes and reads documents

tax Money that you have to pay to the government

territory An area of land that is ruled by a particular leader or group of people

Further reading

**Early Islamic Civilisation
(The History Detective Investigates),**
Claudia Martin (Wayland, 2015)

**Early Islamic Civilisation
(Great Civilisations)**
Anita Ganeri (Franklin Watts, 2014)

Websites

http://www.1001inventions.com/Top7Clocks
Read about seven ingenious clocks from the early Islamic civilisation.

https://www.vam.ac.uk/collections/islamic-middle-east
Explore the V&A Museum's collection of Islamic artefacts.

http://www.crayola.co.uk/free-coloring-pages/islamic-patterns.aspx
Practise colouring in a geometric tile design.

http://www.gohistorygo.com/#!house-of-wisdom/cjsr
Learn more about the House of Wisdom.

Index